1935 if ~~you wanted to~~
read a good ~~book, you needed~~
either a lot of money or a library card.
Cheap paperbacks were available, but their
poor production generally mirrored the quality
between the covers. One weekend that year,
Allen Lane, Managing Director of The Bodley Head,
having spent the weekend visiting Agatha Christie,
found himself on a platform at Exeter station trying to
find something to read for his journey back to London.
He was appalled by the quality of the material he had to
choose from. Everything that Allen Lane achieved from that
day until his death in 1970 was based on a passionate belief
in the existence of 'a vast reading public for *intelligent*
books at a low price'. The result of his momentous vision
was the birth not only of Penguin, but of the 'paperback
revolution'. Quality writing became available for the price of
a packet of cigarettes, literature became a mass medium
for the first time, a nation of book-borrowers became a
nation of book-buyers – and the very concept of book
publishing was changed for ever. Those founding
principles – of quality and value, with an overarching
belief in the fundamental importance of reading –
have guided everything the company has
done since 1935. Sir Allen Lane's
pioneering spirit is still very much alive
at Penguin in 2005. Here's to
the next 70 years!

MORE THAN A BUSINESS

'We decided it was time to end the almost customary half-hearted manner in which cheap editions were produced – as though the only people who could possibly want cheap editions must belong to a lower order of intelligence. We, however, believed in the existence in this country of a vast reading public for intelligent books at a low price, and staked everything on it'
Sir Allen Lane, 1902–1970

'The Penguin Books are splendid value for sixpence, so splendid that if other publishers had any sense they would combine against them and suppress them'
George Orwell

'More than a business ... a national cultural asset'
Guardian

'When you look at the whole Penguin achievement you know that it constitutes, in action, one of the more democratic successes of our recent social history'
Richard Hoggart

Two Stars

PAUL THEROUX

PENGUIN BOOKS

PENGUIN BOOKS

Published by the Penguin Group
Penguin Books Ltd, 80 Strand, London WC2R ORL, England
Penguin Group (USA) Inc., 375 Hudson Street, New York, New York 10014, USA
Penguin Group (Canada), 10 Alcorn Avenue, Toronto, Ontario, Canada M4V 3B2
(a division of Pearson Penguin Canada Inc.)
Penguin Ireland, 25 St Stephen's Green, Dublin 2, Ireland
(a division of Penguin Books Ltd)
Penguin Group (Australia), 250 Camberwell Road, Camberwell, Victoria 3124,
Australia (a division of Pearson Australia Group Pty Ltd)
Penguin Books India Pvt Ltd, 11 Community Centre,
Panchsheel Park, New Delhi – 110 017, India
Penguin Group (NZ), cnr Airborne and Rosedale Roads, Albany,
Auckland 1310, New Zealand (a division of Pearson New Zealand Ltd)
Penguin Books (South Africa) (Pty) Ltd, 24 Sturdee Avenue,
Rosebank 2196, South Africa

Penguin Books Ltd, Registered Offices: 80 Strand, London WC2R ORL, England

www.penguin.com

Published as a Pocket Penguin 2005
1

Copyright © Cape Cod Scriveners Co., 2005
All rights reserved

The moral right of the author has been asserted

Set in 11/13pt Monotype Dante
Typeset by Palimpsest Book Production Limited
Polmont, Stirlingshire
Printed in England by Clays Ltd, St Ives plc

Contents

Author's Note   vii

Starlets   1
Liz in Neverland   9
Marilyn Monroe: The Auction   47

Author's Note

'Liz in Neverland' – my first attempt at a so-called celebrity profile – appeared in a different form in *Talk* magazine. 'Marilyn Monroe: The Auction' – my first visit to a celebrity auction – appeared in *Architectural Digest*. When I was a boy – and even later – these two women represented for me the throbbing epitome of feminine beauty and sexual attraction. Liz was a child star, but Marilyn had begun her career as a starlet. 'Starlets' was my response to a photo essay on the subject by the American photographer Nancy Ellison.

P. T.

Starlets

The starlet first twinkles on a movie screen, in an uncredited role listed on the last crawling titles as, for example, 'Girl in Rowboat', and you think, yawning and stretching and rising to leave the theatre, Which girl? Which rowboat? Only much later in retrospect are you able to match the mature box-office sensation with the simpering young thing fuddling about with a paddle – for it was a paddle not an oar, and a canoe not a rowboat, and the girl a teenage unknown named Marilyn Monroe.

This particular movie (described as forgettable yet I have not forgotten it) was *Scudda-Hoo! Scudda-Hay!* (1948), a starlet vehicle (Natalie Wood and June Haver also appeared), in which Marilyn made her first brief appearance as 'Girl in Rowboat'. I first saw it one summer in the early 1950s in, of all places, St Francis of Assisi Church Hall in Medford, Massachusetts, with hundreds of sweaty pre-teens attending summer school. God knows who chose it for us. It was about mules (the title is derived from the sort of holler a mule team needs as encouragement) – and was also about hayseeds and hicks and farmers' daughters. Perfect viewing for a priapic adolescent on a hot summer afternoon. Marilyn appeared briefly – mere seconds, giggling bare-shouldered in a summer dress in her bobbing boat. It goes without saying that she went on to bigger things, but it is significant that while she was a starlet in this movie she was also posing for nude calendar shots and was already for many men, inside and outside the movie industry, an object of desire – gifted with sexual, rather than acting, talent.

That Marilyn cameo in the mule-team movie seems to me the classic starlet sighting. There are not many starlets in fiction, but their scarcity is compensated for by their vividness. Faye Greener in Nathanael West's Hollywood novel *The Day of the Locust* comes immediately to mind. But the fullest fictional history is that of Margot Peters, the young woman who seduces and ultimately destroys Albinus, the main character in Vladimir Nabokov's black comedy *Laughter in the Dark*. Set in 1920s Berlin, this novel seems to me one of the greatest portraits of a starlet in all literature – greediest, most manipulative, prettiest face, deepest cleavage.

In the opening pages of the novel, in which she works as an usher in a Berlin movie house, 'Margot dreamed of becoming a model, and then a film star. This transition seemed to her quite a simple matter: the sky was there, ready for her star.'

Margot reads biographies of film stars (notably Greta Garbo's) and is constantly talking about her cinematic ambitions. The novel can be dated by a mocking observation Albinus makes about 'the comparative merits of the silent film and the talkie'. 'Sound,' he says, 'will kill the cinema straightaway.'

Margot's dream is the archetypal vision of 'the diamond bright world' of all starlets: 'Margot had only a very vague idea of what she was really aiming at, though there was always that vision of herself as a screen beauty in gorgeous furs being helped out of a gorgeous car by a gorgeous hotel porter under a giant umbrella.' Ultimately she sees herself on screen and is horribly disappointed – appalled by her brief, clumsy appearance: 'Awkward and ugly, with a swollen, leech-black mouth, misplaced brows and unexpected creases in her dress, the girl in the screen stared wildly in front of her . . .'

The novel, a love story that is a rehearsal for and a precursor to *Lolita* (old smitten man, childish wilful lover), also describes betrayal, cruelty, seduction, disillusionment and murder. These horrors are not entirely absent from the classical definition of starletdom, for in any full-coloured description of the starlet she is depicted as a waif, a schemer, a sulky child, a seductress; she is young, she is reckless. She often appears in movies with titles like *The Young and the Reckless*. She is also, so to speak, at risk. The dismembered torso or violated woman in the Hollywood violent-crime story is invariably described in the caption as a starlet.

The starlet's *Look-at-me!* expression gives her the face of a victim, a look of both willingness and reckless innocence. 'I'm yours,' the face seems to say, conveying loveliness and availability, and implying a whole world of carnality. The man of the world smiles inwardly in the knowledge that such a person has got to be a little disturbed, somewhat difficult, vaguely dysfunctional, possessed with the sort of ambition that easily becomes colourful megalomania ('gorgeous furs . . . gorgeous car . . . giant umbrella').

Often the starlet is the sort of star-struck applicant whose waywardness is explained not by men but by other women, who say, 'She's sad, plus she's got real low self-esteem and comes from a real dysfunctional family. I mean, like she was abused by her stepfather.' A director observing such a distracted, needy and manipulative woman is not pitying but hopeful and thinks, Putty in my hands!

'I sucked his cock in Vegas when I was starting out,' a well-known actress whispered to a friend of mine, as a powerful movie executive entered a room in Malibu. Then plaintively added, 'I wonder if he remembers me.'

There is a suggestion of salaciousness in the definition, and the very word 'starlet' even sounds (perhaps unfairly) like 'slut'.

But these are aspects of a definition informed by stereotype, bias, hearsay and the oral tradition, and faulty for that reason. The true definition of a starlet seems impossible to achieve. I consulted eight authoritative – or at least well-known – dictionaries and got almost nowhere. The definitions were vague and sometimes contradictory.

'A promising young performer, esp. a woman' (*Oxford American Dictionary*).

'A young film actress publicized as a future star' (*American Heritage Dictionary of the English Language*).

Same wording but 'represented as a future star' (*Funk & Wagnalls*).

'A young actress who plays small parts in movies and is hoping to become famous' (*Longmans Dictionary of the English Language*).

'*Often disapprovingly.* A starlet is a young actress who hopes to be or is thought likely to be famous in the future' (*Cambridge International Dictionary of English*).

'A young actress – esp. in motion pictures' (*Random House Desk Dictionary*).

'A young movie actress being coached and publicized for starring roles' (*Langenscheidt New College Merriam Webster*).

'A young woman actor billed as a major movie star of the future' (*Encarta World English Dictionary*).

All these definitions contain a grain of truth. 'Often disapprovingly' is the canniest suggestion of all. The word 'star', in the sense of a luminous and celebrated performer, dates from the early nineteenth century. 'Starlet' – which also means 'small star' and is the name for the starfish *asterina* – dates from 1920 (according to *20th Century Words*, by John Ayto), when it first appeared in print in a ditty by one J. Ferguson:

Some 'starlet' sings
Into the footlights glare . . .

Starlets were numerous in the early years of Hollywood. The film historian Ephraim Katz wrote, 'Pretty girls by the hundreds signed on low-paying long-term contracts and were given training, publicity and minor roles in major films, in the hope they would develop into bona fide stars.' And as a sort of epitaph for starlets he concluded, 'Only a few ever made it.'

Verbal descriptions and dictionary definitions are not much use where starlets are concerned. Language fails to do justice to the prettiest face. This has a certain poetic truth, since the received wisdom is that starlets are the least bookish of people, not to say illiterate. This cannot possibly be true, but such a view adds to the appeal, for in the mind of the simple-minded and predatory male a woman's low IQ is part of her beauty. But because a dictionary is little help in, let's say, adumbrating the nuances of the starlet, photographs are a necessity. The starlet is a work in progress, not yet an icon, and great pictures provide all the complex suggestions and associations that are lacking in dictionaries.

Such portraits encapsulate all the possible meanings – the siren, the waif, the girl with screen potential, the babe, the expressive face, the eloquent buttocks. The starlet is depicted with the greatest subtlety in a photographic portrait – not in a walk-on or a cameo in a movie. Some are names in the 'Where are they now?' file. One of the strange conjuring tricks of show business is the transformation that promotes some actresses to glory and makes others vanish without a trace. It is not impossible that some of the women in bygone starlet photographs are at this moment signing up for dieting classes, or twelve-step programmes; or running for public office, or driving their kids in the minivan to soccer practice.

One is reminded that the starlet, typically, is a very young, very pretty, seemingly unaffected and simple girl, until you take a second look and see more complex nuances, some of them worrying, others laudatory. The very pose and facial expressions suggest talent, or its lack. In each face there is hope. In some this hope is conveyed in a sort of job applicant's eagerness to find employment, but in most it is not a simple wish at all but a longing for a career, for a partner, for a life.

Liz in Neverland

It says something for Elizabeth Taylor's much-criticized voice that I could hear it clearly over the loud hack-hack-hack of the helicopter during our ascent at sunset one day over Michael Jackson's Neverland Ranch. Girlish, imploring, screamy, piercing the titanium rotor blades as she was clutching her dog, a Maltese named Sugar, and saying 'Paul, tell the pilot to go around in a circle, so we can see the whole ranch!'

Neverland, the toytown wilderness of carnival rides and doll's houses and zoo animals and pleasure gardens, was dropping beneath us as – characteristically – Elizabeth asked for more.

Even without my relaying the message – even with his ears muffled by headphones – the pilot heard. He lifted us high enough into the peach-coloured sunset so that Neverland seemed even more toylike – lots of twinkling lights looking futile because (apart from the security staff) there were no other humans in sight, only skittish giraffes, and the reptile house with its Frisbee-shaped frogs and fat pythons, where both a cobra and a rattlesnake had smashed their fangs against the glass cage trying to bite me; the ape sanctuary where 'AJ' the big bristly shovel-mouthed

chimp had spat in my face, and Patrick the orang-
utan had tried to twist my hand; the expectorating
llamas, the aggressive swans in the lake, Gypsy the
moody six-ton elephant, which Elizabeth had given
to Michael; the empty fairground rides – Sea Dragon,
the Neverland Dodgems, the Neverland carousel
playing Michael's own song 'Childhood' ('Has anyone
seen my childhood? . . .)'; the large brightly lit railway station; the lawns and flower beds where loud-
speakers disguised as big grey rocks played show
tunes, filling the valley with unstoppable muzak that
drowned the chirping of wild birds. In the middle of
it, a JumboTron the size of a drive-in movie screen
showed a cartoon; two crazy-faced creatures quack-
ing miserably at each other – all of this very bright
in the cloudless dusk, not a soul watching.

'That's the gazebo, where Larry and I tied the
knot,' Elizabeth said, moving her head in an ironiz-
ing wobble. Sugar blinked through prettily combed
white bangs which somewhat resembled Elizabeth's
own lovely white hair. 'Isn't the railway station
darling? Over there is where Michael and I have
picnics,' and she indicated a clump of woods on a
cliff. 'Can we go around one more time?'

Elizabeth is at her most Elizabethan asking for
more. And once again the long scoop of the
Neverland Valley, all 3,000 acres of it, revolved slowly
beneath us, the shadows lengthening from the pinky-
gold glow slipping from the sky.

'The Neverland Movie Theater . . . Flowers . . .

Michael loves flowers,' Elizabeth said. 'Look at the swans on the lake! Whee!'

With swans like that you hardly need Rottweilers, I was thinking. Even though no rain had fallen for months, the acres of lawns watered by underground sprinklers were deep green. Here and there, like toy soldiers, were the uniformed security people, some on foot, others on golf carts, some standing sentry duty; for Neverland is also a fortress.

'Please can we go around just one more time?' Elizabeth said.

'What's that railway station for?' I asked.

'The sick children.'

'And all those rides?'

'The sick children.'

'Look at all those tents.' It was my first glimpse at the collection of tall teepees hidden in the woods.

'The Indian village. The sick children love that place.'

Even from this height I was reminded that this valley of laboriously recaptured childhood was crammed with statuary; lining the gravel roads and the golf-cart paths were little winsome statues of flute players, rows of grateful grinning kiddies, clusters of hand-holding tots, some with banjos, some with fishing rods – and large bronze statues, too, like the centrepiece of the circular drive in front of Neverland's Main House with its dark shingles and mullioned windows, a statue of Mercury (god of merchandise and merchants), rising thirty feet, winged helmet and caduceus and all, balanced on one tippy-toe, the last of the syrupy sunset lingering on his big bronze buttocks, making his bum look like a buttered muffin.

By contrast, the next valley was scattered with cows. We passed over them, and then spun towards the sprawl of Santa Barbara.

'Tell the pilot we want to go low! Lower!'

It was a different voice again, even younger, with the *more please!* pitched as a small girl's squeak. The pilot had heard. He was jerking his thumb up. He brought us past downtown Santa Barbara and over the shore line and almost to the level of the breaking waves.

Elizabeth began to cry out in a shrill little voice, 'Whee! We're skimming! What a rush! Whee!'

Surf was breaking in fat white bolsters releasing feathers of foam two feet below the helicopter's runners. Not far away at the famous Rincon surf break, surfers lollygagging in the line-up on boards waved to us. Startled pelicans flew up as we approached, and they seemed as cinematic and outrageous as Neverland and its JumboTron cartoons and its statues and swans, and its interminable contending music.

Our nearness to the ocean amplified the rotor noise but Elizabeth, undaunted by the racket, was still chatty. She leaned forward and shouted into my ear, 'Have you ever done this before?'

'In Vietnam!' I yelled.

'No – here!' She seemed annoyed, as though I had deliberately contradicted her. 'Sometimes the water hits us! Sometimes we go so low we get wet! Whee!'

The helicopter corkscrewed past Ventura, where we turned inland over the strawberry fields and fruit trees, and then flew east under a dark sky, towards Van Nuys Airport and a waiting limousine.

But Elizabeth was looking back at the western sky and its lingering light.

'It's like a Whistler *Nocturne*,' she said, quietly. The girl's voice was gone. This was a different tone, thoughtful, adult, a little sad, with the characteristic Elizabethan semi-quaver, from a lifetime of lotus-eating. And what struck me was her precise characterization of the sky, perfectly Whistlerish, with blobby light, and ambiguous shadows hovering over the place where Neverland lay.

'So you're Wendy and Michael is Peter?' I had asked a month before, at her house in Bel-Air.

'Yeah. Yeah. There's a kind of magic between us.'

'Magic' had an odd sound in this setting. Upright, her large impressive head and smooth face on a small, much frailer body, she looked like a fugitive chess piece. She is only a few inches taller than five feet. A bad back, three hip operations, a brain tumour, a broken ankle, 'and I fell seventeen times – I was like The Flying Nun!' – all of this in just the past few years, have given her a struggling sideways gait, that too like a peculiar chess move.

Now sipping water, Elizabeth was propped against cushions to favour her back. Her feet in thin slippers were braced against a coffee table on which there was a mass of shattered meteorites – or were they geodes? – forty or more of them with purple crystals glittering in their interior. Behind Elizabeth a wall of masterpieces, cheek by jowl, Van Gogh jammed against Monet, Rouault against Mary Cassatt, Matisse on top of Modigliani, and three Utrillos side by side, past the Tiffany lamp and the table of cut glass and crystal, one piece the size of a coconut. 'From Michael,' Elizabeth explained later. 'He said he wanted to get me the biggest diamond in the world. It's a crystal – isn't it fun? Go on, lift it.' It must have weighed twenty pounds, and its sparkle reached the Frans Hals which was hung over the fireplace, with shelves of bronze horses sculpted by Eliza Todd. The Picasso was over the fish tank. The carpet was white, of the same whiteness as Elizabeth's hair, her slippers, Sugar's fur, most of the furniture. The trophy room was next door, the Michael Jackson portrait in the hall ('To my True Love Elizabeth – I'll love you Forever, Michael'), a Hockney and two Warhols – one a silkscreen icon of Elizabeth – in the library, and four Augustus Johns in, pedantically enough, the john.

It was late afternoon. Elizabeth – a night owl and a notoriously bad sleeper – had not long before risen from her bed, where she had been listening to the Italian singer Andrea Bocelli's album *Romanza*. It would be a normal day – rising in mid-afternoon or so, lots of music, some TV, a turn around the house, a chat with me. A date was planned for later, but nothing special. Rod Steiger was expected. For the past year and a half he has been picking Elizabeth up in his little Honda and taking her out for burgers or fried chicken.

'I was agoraphobic for almost four years,' she said. Medical terms trip off her tongue. 'Didn't leave the house; hardly got out of bed. Rod Steiger got me out of here. He said I was depressed. Then we dated.'

'Dating' is a maddeningly opaque word. In addition to Rod Steiger, who denies any romance, she is currently also dating another man, Cary Schwartz, a Beverly Hills dentist who is in his mid-fifties and accompanied her on her birthday at the Bellagio Hotel in Las Vegas (and to hear Andrea Bocelli) along with his two grown sons, José Eber her hairdresser, Dr Arnie Klein – Michael Jackson's dermatologist – and Michael Jackson himself. Both Dr Klein and José had shown me the commemorative birthday snapshot, all of them beaming at a restaurant table, Michael looking distinctly chalky as he presented Elizabeth with a birthday present, an elephant sculpture, football-sized, covered in jewels. It had been inspired by the big, real, trumpeting elephant, Gypsy, she had given him.

Her friendship with Michael Jackson is something she obviously values but, unlikely as it seems, in the context of her own turbulent life it is almost unremarkable.

'I've had some things happen in my life that people wouldn't *believe*,' she said, apropos of telling me that she could not bear looking back on her life, and would never contemplate an autobiography. 'Because some of it has been so painful, I couldn't relive it. Which is one of the reasons I've avoided psychiatry. I couldn't go back to some of those places and totally relive them. I think I'd go out of my mind.'

A writer sits indoors over the years fantasizing, creating fictional lives, and multiple marriages, and fortunes, and appalling accidents – an exasperating but fairly tidy, risk-free occupation involving paper and pencil. But Elizabeth Taylor – imagination made flesh – has lived out her desires, a series of overlapping lives, with a cast of thousands. But never mind the full life. She has, she claims, even died.

'I went through that tunnel,' she told me, speaking of her tracheotomy operation in 1959 during which she had been pronounced dead. 'I saw the white light and it said, "You have to go back." It actually happened. I didn't talk about it, because I had never heard about it, and I thought, This is Loony Tunes!'

She admits she is the opposite of reflective. Perhaps it is this lack of introspection in her, her unwillingness to look at the past, that accounts for her optimism.

She conceded that, as Mrs Larry Fortensky, she had had to grit her teeth to go to a marriage counsellor. 'But I thought, Why not? I'll try anything.'

Because Larry was acquainted with the counsellor – indeed had seen her before, in the course of one or both of his previous marriages – Elizabeth said, 'They had a conversation which had become a sort of code. I felt left out. But we did it. Got into the car. Did it. Then we wouldn't speak until the next appointment.'

And she laughed, with a peculiar sort of self-mocking mirth that makes her likeable. This fatalistic laugh at her own expense comes after a mention of anything absurdly catastrophic – marital disaster or hospitalization or accident, or the back-from-the-dead story. It puts you at ease; it's subtext is 'I must be mad!' It is also a displacement activity, for the prospect of someone's pity or regret, she says, can reduce her to helpless tears.

What began as a friendship with Michael Jackson has developed into a kind of cause in which she has become almost his only defender.

'What about his' – and I fished for a word – 'eccentricity? Does that bother you?'

'He is magic. And I think all truly magical people have to have that genuine eccentricity.' There is not an atom in her consciousness that allows her the slightest negativity on the subject of Jacko. 'He is one of the most loving, sweet, true people I have ever loved. He is part of my heart. And we would do anything for each other.'

This Wendy with a vengeance, who was a wealthy and world-famous pre-adolescent, supporting her parents from the age of nine, says she easily relates to Michael, who was also a child star and denied a childhood, as well as being viciously abused by his father. There is a 'Katherine' steam engine and a 'Katherine Street' at Neverland; there is no 'Joseph Street', nor anything bearing his father's name.

And Michael, who indulges in obsessive iconography, had for years collected images of Elizabeth Taylor, as he had of Diana Ross and Marilyn Monroe and Charlie Chaplin – and for that matter of Mickey Mouse and Peter Pan, all of whom, over the years in what is less a life than a metamorphosis, he has come physically to resemble. It cannot have escaped Michael's notice that Elizabeth, too, in the almost sixty years of her stardom, has similarly altered; the winsome child has relentlessly morphed from Velvet Brown to Mrs Flintstone, via Cleopatra and the Wife of Bath. Each movie (there are fifty-five – and nine TV films), each marriage (eight), each love affair (about twenty on record) has produced a different face and figure, a new image – while at the same time the woman herself is unchanged: straightforward, funny, truthful, impulsively game ('I'll try anything'), outward-looking, a risk-taker, and somehow still hungry for more.

When out of the blue – they had not yet met – Michael offered her tickets for one of his 'Thriller Tour' concerts at Dodger Stadium she seized them – indeed, she got fourteen tickets. The day was auspicious: 27 February, her birthday and also her son Christopher Wilding's. But the seats were in the glass-enclosed VIP box, a distance from the stage. 'You might as well have been watching it on TV.'

Promising to get a video of the show, she led her large party home.

'Michael called the next day in tears and said, "I'm so sorry. I feel so awful."' He stayed on the line; they talked for two hours. 'And then we talked every day.' Weeks passed; the calls continued. Months went by. 'Really, we got to know each other on the telephone, over three months.'

One day Michael suggested that he might drop by. Elizabeth said fine. He said, 'May I bring my chimpanzee?' Elizabeth said, 'Sure. I love animals.' Michael showed up holding hands with the chimp, Bubbles.

'We have been steadfast ever since,' Elizabeth said. 'I was supposed to go with him on that trip to South Africa.'

'To meet President Mandela?'

'I call him Nelson,' Elizabeth said. 'Because he told me to. Nelson called me and asked me to come with Michael. We chat on the phone. "Hi, Nelson!" Ha ha!'

'Do you see much of Michael?'

'More of him than people realize – more than I realize,' she said. They go in disguise to movies in Westwood and elsewhere, sitting in the back, holding hands. Before I could frame a more particular question, she said, 'Everything about Michael is truthful. And there is something in him that is so dear and childlike – not childish, but childlike – that we both have and identify with.'

She said this in the most adoring Wendy-like way,

but there is in such an apparently sweet manner something of a child taking charge, something defiant, almost despotic.

'I love him. There's a vulnerability inside him, which makes him the more dear,' Elizabeth said. 'We have such fun together. Just playing.'

'Yeah, we try to escape and fantasize,' Michael Jackson told me. 'We have great picnics. It's so wonderful to be with her. I can really relax with her, because we've lived the same life and experienced the same thing.'

'Which is?'

'The great tragedy of childhood stars. And we like the same things. Circuses. Amusement parks. Animals.'

At a prearranged signal he had called me. There was no secretarial intervention of 'Mr Jackson on the line.' The week's supermarket tabloids' headlines were 'Jacko on suicide watch', 'Jacko in loony bin' and, with a South Africa date line, 'Wacko Jacko King of Pop Parasails with 13-year-old.' In fact he was in New York City, where he was recording a new album.

My phone rang and I heard, 'This is Michael Jackson.' The voice was breathy, unbroken, boyish – tentative, yet tremulously eager and helpful. That was its lilting sound, but its substance was denser, like a blind child giving you explicit directions in darkness.

'How would you describe Elizabeth?' I asked.

'She's a warm cuddly blanket that I love to snuggle up to and cover myself with. I can confide in her and trust her. In my business you can't trust anyone.'

'Why is that?'

'Because you don't know who's your friend. Because you're so popular, and there's so many people around you. You're isolated too. Becoming successful means that you become a prisoner. You can't go out and do normal things. People are always looking at what you're doing.'

'Have you had that experience?'

'Oh, lots of times. They try to see what you're reading, and all the things you're buying. They want to know everything. There are always paparazzi downstairs. They invade my privacy. They twist reality. They're my nightmare. Elizabeth is someone who loves me – really loves me.'

'I suggested to her that she was Wendy and you're Peter.'

'But Elizabeth is also like a mother – and more than that. She's a friend. She's Mother Teresa, Princess Diana, the Queen of England, and Wendy.'

He returned to the subject of fame and isolation. 'It makes people do strange things. A lot of our famous luminaries become intoxicated because of it – they can't handle it. And your adrenalin is at the zenith of the universe after a concert – you can't sleep. It's maybe two in the morning and you're wide awake. After coming off stage you're floating.'

'How do you handle that?'

'I watch cartoons – I love cartoons. I play video games. Sometimes I read.'

'You mean you read books?'

'Yeah. I love to read short stories and everything.'

'Any in particular?'

'Somerset Maugham,' he said quickly, and then, pausing at each name, 'Whitman. Hemingway. Twain.'

'What about those video games?'

'I love *X-Man. Pinball. Jurassic Park.* The martial-arts ones – *Mortal Kombat.*'

'I played some of the video games at Neverland. There was an amazing one called *Beast Buster.*'

'Oh, yeah, that's great. I pick each game. That one's maybe too violent, though. I usually take some with me on tour.'

'How do you manage that? The video-game machines are pretty big, aren't they?'

'Oh, we travel with two cargo planes.'

'Have you written any songs with Elizabeth in mind?'

'"Childhood".'

'Is that the one with the line "Has anyone seen my childhood?"?'

'Yes. It goes,' and he liltingly recited, '"Before you judge me, try to . . ."' (he recited six lines).

'Didn't I hear that playing on your merry-go-round at Neverland?'

Delightedly, he said, 'Yes! Yes!'

We talked about the famous Neverland wedding, about Larry, whom Michael said he liked. About Elizabeth as an inspiration, and their mutual friend Carole Bayer Sager, who had written some of the songs on the *Off The Wall* album. About childhood, and how Elizabeth used to support her family when she was a young girl.

'I did that too. I was a child supporting my family. My father took the money. Some of the money was put aside for me, but a lot of the money was put back into the entire family. I was just working the whole time.'

'So you didn't have a childhood, then – you lost it. If you had it to do again how would you change things?'

'Even though I missed out on a lot I wouldn't change anything.'

'I can hear your little kids in the background.' The gurgling had become insistent, like a plughole in flood. 'If they wanted to be performers and lead the life you led, what would you say?'

'They can do whatever they want to do. If they want to do that, it's okay.'

'How will you raise them differently from the way you were raised?'

'With more fun. More love. Not so isolated.'

'Elizabeth says she finds it painful to look back on her life. Do you find it hard to do that?'

'No, not when it's pertaining to an overview of your life rather than any particular moment.'

This oblique and somewhat bookish form of expression was a surprise to me – another Michael Jackson surprise. He had made me pause with 'intoxicated' and 'zenith of the universe' too. I said, 'I'm not too sure what you mean by "overview".'

'Like childhood. I can look at that. The arc of my childhood.'

'But there's some moment in childhood when you feel particularly vulnerable. Did you feel that? Elizabeth said that she felt she was owned by the studio.'

'Sometimes really late at night we'd have to go out – it might be three in the morning, to do a show. My father made us. He would get us up. I was seven or eight. Some of these were clubs or private parties at people's houses. We'd have to perform.' This was in Chicago, New York, Indiana, Philadelphia, he added – all over the country. 'I'd be sleeping and I'd hear my father. "Get up! There's a show!"'

'But when you were onstage, didn't you get a kind of thrill?'

'Yes. I loved being onstage. I loved doing the shows.'

'What about the other side of the business – if someone came up after the show, did you feel awkward?'

'I didn't like it. I've never liked people-contact. Even to this day, after a show, I hate it, meeting people. It makes me shy. I don't know what to say.'

'But you did that Oprah interview, right?'

'With Oprah it was tough. Because it was on TV – on TV it's out of my realm. I know that everyone is looking and judging. It's so hard.'

'Is this a recent feeling – that you're under scrutiny?'

'No,' he said firmly, 'I have always felt that way.'

'Even when you were seven or eight?'

'I'm not happy doing it.'

'Which I suppose is why talking to Elizabeth over a period of two or three months on the phone would be the perfect way to get acquainted. Or doing what we're doing right now.'

'Yes.'

At some point Michael's use of the phrase 'lost childhood' prompted me to quote the line from Leon Bloy 'In the lost childhood of Judas, Jesus was betrayed,' and I heard 'Wow!' at the other end of the line. He asked me to explain what that meant, and when I did he urged me to elaborate. What sort of a childhood did Judas have? What had happened to him? Where had he lived? Who had he known? Twenty minutes of biblical apocrypha with Michael Jackson ensured, and well over an hour later we talked about his plan to perform in Honolulu for a Millennium concert, and the progress of his album.

We returned to the subject of Elizabeth. He told me what a pleasure it had given him to take her and her entourage to Las Vegas – to give her the jewelled elephant. I said I had seen a snapshot of the birthday party.

'That was great. It's the way we really are. We go out and have fun.'

Given Elizabeth's past, her insisting to Oprah 'Michael is the least weird man I have ever known' is not the hyperbolic statement it sounds. She was put down as credulous at the time, but it is a clever rebuttal, and it is a fact that she has known – been married to, had affairs with, been mixed up with – some of the weirdest, most abusive, addictive, profligate, polymorphously perverse men imaginable: drunks, brutes, even convicted felons. Henry Wynberg, one of her lovers, was busted for fiddling with the odometers of the second-hand cars he was selling. Elizabeth first got into the perfume business with Wynberg.

She was slapped around by Nicky Hilton, cheated on by Richard Burton, bad-mouthed by Eddie Fisher. She sold a 69-carat diamond and her purple Rolls to help get John Warner into the Senate. And Larry Fortensky – poor, beer-swilling Larry, who was treated to his first ride in a plane and his first foreign country by Elizabeth – Larry, you gather, might use some of his $2 million settlement to pay for a course in anger management. And then there are the lovers, who reputedly range from Max Lerner to Ryan O'Neal, with Carl Bernstein, Bob Dylan and a former Iranian ambassador somewhere in there too.

Next to this bunch, Michael – who claims not to smoke, drink or take drugs – must truly seem to her like Peter Pan. He is famous for his whisper. 'Whee!' is one of his trademark expressions too. His generosity towards this woman, who adores receiving presents, makes him as much her patron as her playmate; though it is as playmates that she describes the relationship.

But it seemed to me that every relationship of Elizabeth's involved her in a sort of role-playing, as though a marriage was a movie, with a beginning, middle and end. And each different movie – with a different leading man, different costumes and locations and story points – had a different 'look', as though an inventive art director had had a hand in the design. Looking over the decades of photographs there is a startling dissimilarity in the Elizabeths – the fresh young all-American Mrs Hilton, the English Mrs Wilding, the Jewish Mrs Todd, the stage wife Mrs Fisher, the much louder and somewhat Welsh Mrs Burton, the podgy political campaigner Mrs Warner, and finally the svelte Mrs Fortensky in a leather jacket and jeans, famous for showing up, looking terrific, at Larry's construction sites. Even for lovers her look changed – deeply tanned on the arm of George Hamilton, somewhat of a moll next to Wynberg, and, with slick Hispanic hair, in a ruffled polka-dot dress with her Mexican lover, Victor Luna.

Some of the marriages were melodramas, a few tragedies, with a farce and a comedy or two. Nicky Hilton – young, rich, drunken, wasteful – was straight out of an F. Scott Fitzgerald script. The Wilding effort – with a transplanted English actor wilting in Los Angeles – was an Anglo-American culture clash. The short intense Todd marriage, tragically ending in a plane wreck, had a sequel, with music – the marriage to Todd's friend Eddie Fisher, a farcical and faltering lounge-act movie about failure and pills. The Burton business was a two-parter, with serious drinking and spending, highly emotional, complex and passionate, proving Freud's dictum that in all love affairs four people are involved. One of her Utrillos depicts a chateau in Switzerland near where she says she secretly met Burton after the filming of *Cleopatra*: she values the painting less for its being a masterpiece than for recalling the scene of what she says was one of the most romantic moments with one of her two great loves (the other being Todd). The last pair of marriages – to the rising politician John Warner, to truck-driver Larry – amounted to comedy, with all the excruciating pain that true comedy requires.

Wifehood as a role? Marriages as movies? I decided to ask her.

One night, just before going out to meet Elizabeth, I saw John Warner on television, talking about the war in Kosovo. He is the chairman of the Senate Armed Services Committee, but even the most charitable assessment of the senator makes him seem doltish and vain – unpersuasive, self-important, with his closely set eyes and narrow skull giving him the ingratiating face of a spaniel.

Speaking about the John Warner marriage she said, 'It seemed to me that if I didn't get out of it soon I'd go crazy – out of that situation where you have no opinion of your own, just the candidate's wife.'

'That's like a movie title, *The Candidate's Wife*,' I

said, and asked her whether her own marriages had seemed that way, so specific and so unreal at the same time.

Elizabeth considered this, then said, 'You don't start a movie expecting it to crash. You get married expecting it to be for ever. That's why you get married.'

But that was not my point; it wasn't a matter of intention, but rather that the result had been so cinematic. It seemed to me that a child star, trained for the changing demands of specific circumstances, was perfectly suited for a life of endless adaptation, of multiple roles. Of course no one entered a marriage expecting it to end, but in fact all her marriages had ended, all her love affairs had crashed.

Elizabeth was of course the wrong person to ask about this, and yet everything she told me made it seem as though her marriage, *The Candidate's Wife*, was infinitely more watchable than the movies she made around this period, *A Little Night Music*, *Winter Kills*, *The Mirror Crack'd* and *Return Engagement*.

'I had to go along with the party line,' Elizabeth said. 'I was told I was not allowed to wear purple. The Republican Women's Committee said, "It denotes royalty."

'I said, "*So?*"

'"And it denotes passion."

'I said, "What's the matter with that?"

'They said, "You're the candidate's wife!"'

Cut.

Elizabeth bought herself a conservative suit – 'I hate suits!' – and campaigned for the next two months, five or six places a day, no time to eat, the candidate frenetically stumping for votes, the candidate's wife smiling bravely. One day on their way to a Republican function they enter the building through a rear entrance, candidate and wife hurrying. Passing a tray of food, Candidate Warner – whose pet name for his wife was 'Pooters' – said, 'There's some fried chicken right there, Pooters. Grab some fried chicken, and get a breast or something down into your stomach. This is the last chance for us to eat for the rest of the day!'

'So I grabbed a breast,' Elizabeth said, 'and all of a sudden – *aargh!* You know those two-and-a-half-inch bones? One of them got stuck in my throat. John Belushi did a whole sketch on it, on *Saturday Night Live*, the bastard! Choking on a chicken bone in Little Gap, Virginia!'

In a bizarre improvisation of first aid, Elizabeth snatched a bread roll, broke it in half and 'swallowed half of it to push [the bone] down further – because evidently I was changing colours'.

This did not work. Elizabeth was taken to the hospital, and, warming to her theme as she told the story, she described how the doctor took a long rubber hose and stuck it down her throat. 'To get the bone into my stomach – with no anaesthetic, not so much as an aspirin – and they got it into my stomach. But the jokes! I was teased for a year!'

After Warner was elected, a luncheon was given for Elizabeth by the Republican ladies to thank her for her contribution to the victory. Little did they know how great the contribution had been – Elizabeth had sold one of Burton's more extravagant gifts, 'my great big 69-carat diamond . . . to maintain my half of the marriage'.

For the luncheon, 'I took my purple Halston pants suit out of mothballs – had it all spruced up – and wore it in all my glory. I said, "Judy" – she was the manager of the campaign – "I'm wearing this in your honour!"'

Were this a film, this scene would have been the high point, towards the middle, with the later action suggested in something Elizabeth said to me: 'As the candidate's wife I found it very hard to keep my mouth shut.' Warner was now in the Senate. Elizabeth was redundant. 'Washington is the cruellest city for a woman in the world.' She was idle. He was, she says, obsessed with showing up for the Roll Call Vote; he wanted to record his perfect attendance. And he succeeded. 'He was 100 per cent on his Roll Call Vote. "John Warner?" "Aye!"' From this exertion in the Senate he returned home exhausted.

'And he'd say, "Why don't you pour yourself a Jack Daniels, Pooters, and go on upstairs and watch TV."

'So Pooters would pour herself a large Jack Daniels and go upstairs and watch TV and wait for another day. And on and on. And I thought, My Jack Daniels are getting larger and larger, and if I don't get my finger out I'm going to drink myself either to death or in such a stupor that there is going to be no life for me.'

At this low point in Washington, melodramatic and self-mocking in Elizabeth's telling, she thought, 'What is the most challenging thing I can think of to do in the world, the most difficult to me physically, mentally – but within the realm of possibility? Ah, do a Broadway play!'

Against the advice of nearly everyone she knew, she settled on *The Little Foxes*. 'I went to a fat farm, to lose weight and get some energy back – stop drinking, feel good about myself. Took the script with me.'

Rehearsals were in Florida, and though Warner didn't show up for opening night Tennessee Williams did – he had told Elizabeth he had always thought of her as 'a Tennessee Williams heroine' and she proved it playing his heroines in *Cat on a Hot Tin Roof*, *Suddenly Last Summer* and *Sweet Bird of Youth*. She says that she felt liberated by *The Little Foxes*; she liked the theatre people and the applause and the family atmosphere of a show. This play went on the road, and so did Elizabeth in every sense. She was soon divorced from Warner but continuing with the London run of the play.

It is the perfect ending to *The Candidate's Wife*. The star who has forsaken acting to assume the real-life role of the wife of a rising politician finds that she is superfluous after he gets elected. Seeing that she is dying as a Washington wife, she chooses freedom by getting herself a part in a play, another role-within-a-role. She can only be herself and 'feel freedom and joy' by acting.

And then the actress who is liberated by the play falls for Tony Geary, a soap-opera star, and she makes a number of guest appearances in the TV series *General Hospital*.

Life to life, role to role. Ten years pass, and the next movie is *The Trucker's Wife*. The jewels are gone; Elizabeth is in jeans, the adoring spouse of a mono-syllabic blue-collar worker named Larry. He has never been in an airplane; he has never set foot outside the United States. 'I got such a vicarious kick out of taking him to places that I had never gone to, so that I wouldn't have an advantage over him and that we could share the newness together.' She takes him for his airplane rides – to Morocco, to Thailand. Because they are the guests of the Thai royal family they have a motorcycle escort. There are never any other cars in view when they are on the road; the roads are cleared of all traffic for them. Larry, in his innocence, believes all foreign travel is like this, empty roads and saluting policemen; but he hates foreign food. He is bored. 'He always wanted to go to McDonald's, wherever we were.'

Back home in Bel-Air, 'I used to get up at four in the morning and have breakfast with him. After Larry went to work, I went back to bed. Then he would come home and it was wonderful – he was sweaty, he had dirty hands, he was beautiful, and he played with his [homing] pigeons.

'I was so proud of him for working. I was kind of hurt when he stopped.'

And when Larry the trucker stopped working, and began drinking, his famous temper sometimes flared. Idle, there was only daytime TV and beer for him. It could only end with the trucker's departure from Bel-Air. End of movie.

Far from belittling these doomed love affairs by comparing them to movies, I felt Elizabeth warranted praise for putting her heart and soul into them, for throwing herself into the role of spouse with such gusto. By changing roles she has kept her vitality, though Sheridan Morley observed to me how she was like a certain sort of character in a Henry James novel, 'innocent, yet at the centre of death and destruction'.

With the exception of Eddie Fisher ('Let's say we're not exactly intimate buds'), she remained fairly close to all her ex-husbands. And while she pokes fun at them, she is never unkind; if there is abuse, she lets the facts speak for themselves.

'It's a mixed blessing, discovering boys,' she said, after a long pleasurable recollection of her riding horses as a young girl. In the beginning there were two or three strictly chaperoned romances, and then, after a short courtship, she and Nicky Hilton were married. 'I was a virgin – I was half-hearted. That was a foolish thing, let me tell you.'

Her voice became drier, and she quailed slightly, crouching on the sofa, seeming almost physically to contract, as she continued, 'He started drinking two weeks after we got married. I thought he was a nice pure all-American boy. Two weeks later, *wham! bam!* All the physical abuse started. I left him after nine months of marriage . . . after,' and she paused and looked into the middle distance, 'having a baby kicked out of my stomach.'

'That's terrible,' I said.

'He was drunk. I thought, This is not why I was put on earth. God did not put me here to have a baby kicked out of my stomach. I had terrible pains. I saw the baby in the toilet. I didn't know that I was pregnant, so it wasn't a malicious or on-purpose kind of act. It just happened.'

Without another word, she got up, holding herself, and left the room. Some minutes passed before she returned, saying that the memory had given her physical pains in her abdomen. She said, 'I have never spoken about this before,' and changed the subject, to Montgomery Clift, how she found him his first lover.

How had she known that Monty was gay?

'I don't know how I knew. I loved Monty with all my heart, but I knew there would never be a romance for us. No one had explained it to me, but I knew it. Monty was in the closet and I think I knew what he was fighting. He was tormented his whole life. I tried to explain to him that it wasn't awful. It was the way that Nature had made him.'

If there is a constant in her endlessly altering life, it is the friendship of gay men. Husbands and lovers have come and gone but there has always been a gay man – and usually more than one – acting as an escort, confidant, friend, almost sister. Roddy McDowall was a friend from 1942 when they appeared in *Lassie Come Home* until his death in 1998. Montgomery Clift. James Dean. Rock Hudson. Tennessee Williams. Halston. Malcolm Forbes. Andy Warhol. Truman Capote. Actors, directors, dress designers, hairdressers, writers, nearly all of them adoring and, even she admits, among the closest friends she has in her life. Her lovers have been abusive, but there is not a recorded instance of even a spat with one of her gay friends.

When AIDS began to claim the lives of some of them she reacted. A near martyr to hedonistic self-indulgence seems only at first sight to be a poor candidate for good works; in fact a life of rampant sexual excess and living large is the usual apprenticeship for the moral crusader, the object of self-denial being, very often, simple atonement. Shocked by these AIDS deaths, Elizabeth distinguished herself by calling attention to them and being the first person in Hollywood to raise money for AIDS research, first with the American Federation for AIDS Research (AMFAR) and also with Elizabeth Taylor AIDS Foundation.

'If you're famous there's so many good things you can do,' she told me. 'If you do something worthwhile you feel better. I spent my whole last fifty years protecting my privacy. I thought, Wait, you're getting angry – you can turn your fame around and use it for something positive. I resented my fame until I realized I could use it.'

In the beginning of the AIDS outbreak, people 'were getting bent out of shape – getting angry and hateful. They weren't doing anything. I got so upset.'

She hosted the first AIDS fund-raiser in Hollywood, a landmark event in 1985, much to the horror of people in the industry who had tried to conceal the fact that anyone in Hollywood was gay. That fund-raiser was a success. Many more have followed.

'I am this dreaded famous person. I can get under their skin,' Elizabeth says. She has always rather liked the idea that she has been rebellious, and it was also a way to make rebellion work. Her efforts have earned so much money for AIDS research – some $150 million – that even the most sceptical bystanders admit that she has made a profound difference to AIDS research by raising the money to develop the life-extending protease inhibitor.

She is still at it. The Cannes Film Festival is an occasion to dress up and play the star, but it is also an occasion to host an AMFAR dinner. She was doing this a few months ago (in May 2000). She raised $2.6 million on that night. In her speech, she urged the potential donors to 'kick ass'.

'That's why I do photo shoots – to keep my fame alive. So people won't say, "Who's that broad?"'

She laughs about Hollywood fame, how it has

changed since she was a child star. 'Being under contract was heinous.' It was the sort of thing that Michael Jackson easily related to. As Elizabeth describes it, 'Being loaned out for $500,000 and getting $5,000 a week, which really pissed me off – excuse me! – it just wasn't fair.'

But, in spite of the independence and the big money, there is something missing in Hollywood today. It is not the star system, though Elizabeth can be said to be the last star. It is not even the decline of the studios and the rise of the independent film-makers. Not the scandals and the marriages and murders – there are still some of those. What is it?

'There's no tits any more,' Elizabeth said. 'And if there are, they're fake balloons. I mean, you can spot them a mile off. It's all become slightly androgynous. That's not very sexy.'

'So Hollywood's titless these days – that's the message?' I said. 'But I don't want to put words in your mouth.'

Laughing, she said, 'Didn't I say that?'

That evening Rod Steiger showed up, driving a little Honda, wearing sneakers. Shaven head, square shoulders, wearing black, he could have been Mussolini on an off day, paying a call on Clara Petacci. Sunk in depression, Steiger had not been able to work for eight years and was very nearly broke when, with medication and doctoring, he began acting again. A year and a half ago he visited Elizabeth, whom he hardly knew, to propose that she appear with him in

Somewhere – a script he co-wrote – a sequel, Oz re-visited, all the characters grown older. In this version, Elizabeth would play the older Dorothy. But Steiger was shocked at the sight of her – he saw her as blue and housebound, if not clinically depressed and agoraphobic, and, having been through the same things himself, he decided to make her his mission. He insisted that they go out together, and he kept up the pressure for her to socialize. And so Elizabeth was returned to the world. Steiger wrote a poem about Elizabeth, called 'The Price' – the price she has paid for the life she has led. Steiger, who sees her as 'an enchantress who has become a victim of her powers to enchant', says, 'She'll go anywhere for fresh air.'

Michael Jackson is fresh air. Perhaps her ultimate film is the one she is enacting with him now – truer to the spirit of her life than Steiger's *Wizard of Oz* update. There are two books on the coffee table in the library of Michael's house at Neverland, *Peter Pan* and a picture book, Michael's own *HIStory*. The house is full of Peter Pan iconography. Almost consciously, Elizabeth and Michael are role-playing in a sequel to Barrie's book, but *Peter and Wendy* in their version is stranger, more highly coloured, more complete, and longer running than any of the marriage movies that I had animadverted upon with a reluctant Elizabeth in Bel-Air – and *The Crooner's Wife*, *The Candidate's Wife*, *The Trucker's Wife* and the others have much less potential than this one about Wendy grown older and the reclusive refusing-to-age Peter. There is no conflict, nor any likelihood of it; no sex, no struggle, no deprivation. I had the impression they hug a lot and share confidences. It is all about lost childhood, secret pleasures, picnics, food fights and instant gratification. If they crave an elephant or a concert or a game or a jet plane to take them away, they have it immediately. For their purposes the Neverland Ranch is perfect: the girlish mother, the boyishly patron-like son, the frisson of sex existing in the pulses of the air – the touching, holding, teasing, hugging, life as play and plenty of money. Even pirates! Already, *Peter and Wendy* has shown that it has legs: this friendship has lasted longer than any of Elizabeth's actual marriages.

Elizabeth had an appetite for life, and 'appetite' was the word that kept occurring to me when I thought of her: it meant zest, and also a hunger which was somehow never satisfied. In this hunger she is at her most Elizabethan. Of course this is a metaphor, but she is not a metaphorical person – her feet are squarely on the ground, she is literal-minded, and her appetite is literally that, a desire to devour. She has said many times that when she was fat it was not a result of unhappiness – it was that she loved to eat. And she adored the most fattening foods – ice cream, fried chicken. Steiger brings her hot dogs from a joint in Malibu; the dentist takes her out for burgers.

Everyone who has known her (and many who haven't) has something to say about the way she has lived her life. Most of these stories are about her being fabulous, about excess, her nine lives, her accidents, her ailments; many about the oddity of her being at the centre of so much catastrophe. Mike Nichols, who directed her in his first film, and one of Elizabeth's best, *Who's Afraid of Virginia Woolf,* has been the most succinct: 'There are three things I never saw her do: tell a lie, be unkind, or arrive on time.'

Though Elizabeth says she examines nothing in her life or behaviour, her unpunctuality is the richest of the many aspects that repay scrutiny. Her lateness amounts almost to a title, Her Serene Lateness. There is a lateness story associated with everything she has ever done, and this is in itself extraordinary, for she has apparently never done anything on time. Her film career began when she was ten, but that was, metaphorically speaking, the only recorded instance of her ever having been early.

Lateness is a theme in her life, as illness importantly is, and yet they are not related. Illness does not explain her unpunctuality, and even 'unpunctuality' is a lame word for her chronic and incurable condition of reluctance and delay, which verges on the despotic, if not the pathological. We all know, and in our hearts resent, people who are habitually late. Thinking about Elizabeth, I realized what a rich subject this is, one deserving a monograph if not a whole textbook, as dense as a book might be on the subject of the manipulative personality or spousal abuse – two areas that lateness overlaps with, because it is not a solitary affliction, but rather one that involves at least two people, the latecomer and the waiter. In Elizabeth's case the waiter might be me in her living room, or many hundreds of people in a theatre wondering when the curtain is going to rise on *The Little Foxes*, or a thousand people on the set of *Cleopatra* awaiting her arrival, or John Warner tapping his foot on his wedding day, for she was late to that event too. In the theatre, the curtain has been held. Directors have raged in vain. Heads of state, Queen Elizabeth II, the Pope, her closest friends – no one has been privileged to see her on time. She is impartially unpunctual. What about airplanes? I asked a person who some-times travels with her. Planes have take-off slots and flight plans, and must leave on the minute. But, many times, commercial flights have been held for her. Was your plane unaccountably late in taking off from LAX? Chances are that Elizabeth had a seat in First and someone made a call.

That habitual lateness involves a neurotic sense of entitlement, and a bid for power, is perhaps obvious. It raises the ante in a relationship. It is a consistent feature in courtship and sexuality – the aroused person is made to wait, the act is delayed until the loved one appears, and even then there is delay until the Seventh Veil is dropped. 'Meet me in the dress-ing room – we'll make love,' ran a stripper's line in a seedy show I saw as a youth in Boston's Scollay Square. 'If I'm late, start without me.'

Lateness is a diva's trait, allowing her to make an entrance. It is also classically passive-aggressive. The narcissism in lateness is undeniable, and what makes this egocentric demand absurd is the latecomer's expectation that you will be on time. It is not really a contradiction. A late person obviously places a high value on punctuality: everything must begin the moment the latecomer arrives; the latecomer is never made to wait – this is one of the demands of lateness. When Elizabeth arrives the curtain goes up, the camera rolls, the pictures are snapped, the music plays, the show begins. No one else must be late. I was privy to Elizabeth saying, 'If he is not here in fifteen minutes, then fuck him – I'll never see him again.'

No one has ever said that of her. She expects to be taken on her own terms, so her lateness functions as a sort of test. If you are not willing to wait for her she is not interested in you. You must never expect her to wait for you; you must always be on time, despite knowing that she will not be. What right have you to be late? But for her it is a privilege, a flourish that functions as a reminder in everything she has done. To say it is a queenly attribute is probably wrong, since royalty are notorious time-keepers. It is more characteristic of the ball-breaker, the manipulator, the control freak, someone deeply insecure. It is the trait of the bullying man, the coquette and the cock-teaser, the person needing reassurance, anyone who wishes to assert control. You must wait for me; I will never wait for you.

What puzzled me was – given the fact that she is not in films any more, that her workload is light, that she doesn't read, that she has little more to occupy her mind than her dates and her dog – what on earth is she doing when she is not where she is supposed to be? Like a little girl, Elizabeth disingenuously apologized for being late when we met, and I always made a point of asking her what she had been doing. 'I was upstairs – singing and dancing,' carried away by the music of Andrea Bocelli, she told me once. But she also fusses endlessly, changes her clothes – her whole outfit – adjusts her make-up, kicks off her shoes and tries others, dithers over her jewellery, cuddles Sugar, talks on the phone.

This deeply dislikable quality ends friendships, but of course, since it is designed to test friendships, that is inevitable. In Elizabeth it is an accepted mode of behaviour, on a par with a handicap, as though she is a figure worthy of sympathy, like a limper or a twitcher – in her case someone seriously time-challenged. But I saw it as another detail in the ongoing drama of *Peter and Wendy*, for most of all it is a trait of the troubled child, who is often a foot-dragger without really knowing the deeper reason, and in the case of the foot-dragging child there always is a deeper reason.

It is an Elizabethan characteristic, but it does not sum her up. Writing this story I was able to spend enough time with her to see her at her most Elizabethan, at that moment – like the moment in a movie – when so much is revealed by a look or a line.

There was the shocking business about Nicky Hilton – but less the revelation than her getting up just afterwards and haltingly leaving the room, her hands against her stomach, undoubtedly in physical pain.

And at Neverland, in Michael's dining room, a much lighter moment, when she was with the chef and debating what to eat. She finally settled on a big cheese omelette, with ketchup, but as she was tucking into it she saw someone else with a plate of french fries – the twiggy frozen Mickey D. kind – and she said with real gusto in a hungry voice, 'Hey, where did you get those!' And in minutes she too had a big plate of fries.

'Please, God, supersize my life' has always been Elizabeth's prayer, as eating has always been an Elizabethan theme. There is a story of Elizabeth looking in a friend's refrigerator and speaking fondly to the food she saw on the shelves, saying, 'I'm going to eat you . . . and then I'm going to eat you . . . and then I'm going to eat you . . .'

One day she was telling me, very slowly, with real feeling, about a photo shoot she had done for her line of White Diamonds perfume – an enterprise which has assured her a substantial income and eliminated the necessity ever to act again.

'I had on a 101-carat diamond,' she said, pausing after each word. She licked her lips and there was a chuckle of pleasure in her throat. 'No flaws!' And, again pausing between the words, 'Talk about a rush!'

She clutched her finger on which the imaginary emerald-cut diamond ring was fitted, and a shudder of hunger shook her small brittle body as she lifted the finger to her mouth and said with a shout that barely concealed a shriek, 'I wanted to swallow it!'

Another day she was listening to a Bocelli ballad and singing along, then interrupted herself and said, '*Piu! Piu!* I love *piu*! What does *piu* mean?'

'It means "more",' I said.

'*Piu!*'

The essential Elizabeth I was not privileged to observe, but I had it on good authority. After a particularly good session of talk with her at her house, I went away. Soon after, speaking with a mutual friend, Elizabeth said, 'Is Paul married?'

Marilyn Monroe: The Auction

There is a powerful element of fetishism in any auction of celebrity memorabilia, but this was fetishism in its highest form, and at the highest prices. In the brilliant spotlight, isolated on a pedestal, beautiful and absurd, Lot 2 glittered like a surrealist's 'found object' – a pair of red stiletto-heeled shoes. Rubious and very pretty, of course, yet no more than women's shoes. Staring fixedly at these shoes were a thousand eager faces. Superficially elegant, the atmosphere in Christie's main sale room in New York was in fact much more visceral, even outlandish, and as dramatic as a cargo-cult veneration of sacred totems.

Everyone in the room wanted those shoes, for they had been invested with the spirit of Marilyn Monroe, whose life was being celebrated and also re-evaluated. The bidders in front of me, an older woman and a young couple, were conferring suavely in Italian, and, when the bidding began, it was the woman who matched and raised all comers. The bidding rose quickly from ten thousand to twenty thousand and progressed through the thirties. The older woman was unfazed, and even at forty thousand she was briskly nodding.

'Forty-two thousand dollars,' the auctioneer, Lord

Hindlip, crowed, and repeated, and a moment later, when the shoes were hers, the woman murmured, '*Sono contenta*' – 'I'm happy.' She was Signora Ferragamo, her son Massimo seated next to her. The red shoes also were Ferragamos.

The next lot was a pair of rhinestone earrings (actual value perhaps $50). Frantic bidding got them to $21,000. Four lots later, a small stack of denim blue jeans. In the second row, the designer Tommy Hilfiger indicated an interest. After considerable opposition, more than might be expected to secure a pair of unstylish, faded, crumpled thrift-shop jeans, last seen stretched upon Marilyn's incomparable body in the 1954 movie *River of No Return*, Mr Hilfiger got them for $35,000.

Those were the lower-priced items. The white piano (an authentic relic from Marilyn's childhood), bought by Marilyn's mother from the actor Federic March, went for $600,000 – and the buyer was later revealed to be the singer Mariah Carey. The DiMaggio wedding band went for $700,000; the sparkly dress known as the 'Happy Birthday, Mr President' dress was bought for $1,267,500, a world auction record for a woman's dress.

This auction, 'The Personal Property of Marilyn Monroe', a name more suggestive than sonorous, was one of the grandest examples of pure theatre I have ever witnessed. After months of publicity, and a European tour of the choicest items, Marilyn Monroe's effects were sold in New York at this dramatic event spread over two days. The ballroom-sized auction room was packed: a mass of seated bidders and spectators, bright-faced with eagerness and dressed as though for a party; a hundred employees standing, holding telephones; at the back, a bank of television cameras, sixty or more, trained on the people and the lots as they were exhibited.

The items were spiritedly bid upon, yet behind those 576 lots was a sorry story of one of the loveliest, and unhappiest, women who ever lived. The auction said everything about the mute pathos of material objects, the sadness of used goods; about Hollywood, and American life; about Marilyn.

Her life was short and, except for a few sunny periods, mostly miserable. Her single mother was mentally ill and committed to an asylum. The girl born as Norma Jean spent her early years shunting among eleven foster homes and an orphanage, the Los Angeles Orphans' Home. She was still only eleven. The next four years she spent with a legal guardian, Grace McKee, who brokered her first marriage, a few weeks after Norma Jean, who had already left school, turned sixteen. She called her husband 'Daddy'. Later, DiMaggio was 'Pa', Arthur Miller was 'Pops' – and she would sing with feeling 'My Heart Belongs to Daddy'. Not surprisingly she was unsure of her true father's identity. She was just twenty when she was first divorced, took the name Marilyn Monroe, and auditioned for movies.

She made three attempts at suicide before she was

twenty-five, and several serious ones later, including an overdose in 1957 when married to Arthur Miller. She had a self-destructive streak, and wilfulness and melancholy characterized her fragmented personality, so that none of the marriages satisfied her; nor did any of her many love affairs. Her life was Hollywood writ large, for she was a talented actress and more intelligent than she was perceived to be. Her suicide in 1962, at the age of thirty-seven, shocked America. She died with $5,000 in the bank. All her personal effects were bequeathed not to her mother, Gladys, who was still alive at the time of Marilyn's death, but to her sometime acting coach, Lee Strasberg. These effects – everything she owned, down to the last potholder and cheap ashtray and Mexican hat ('Isla Margarita' stitched on the brim) – were expertly wrapped and put into storage. Lee Strasberg has been described as an opportunist and a Svengali, and even Strasberg's son John has said of Marilyn, 'The greatest tragedy was that people, even my father in a way, took advantage of her.' With the death of Strasberg, the Marilyn Monroe paraphernalia, still cached, ultimately became the sole property of Strasberg's second wife, Anna, who had never met Marilyn. Instead of keeping the items together in a permanent collection – for they are tiny, and only as an assemblage do the pieces of a mosaic make a picture – the widow Strasberg decided to auction them. It is she who will get the lion's share of the proceeds of the Christie's auction, of almost $13.5 million. It is important to stress that Marilyn was not a collector of anything valuable. She wasn't rich, she was evidently frugal, and these objects, the material part of her life, were anything but trophies. They were the things she actually used: her toaster, her tables and chairs, her books, her TV, her dresses and shoes, her knick-knacks and cheap mementoes, her inexpensive jewellery, and, most revealing of all, annotated scripts and scribbled notepads.

What do you know of a person from their effects? Generally speaking, very little when it is a selection of jewellery or paintings. This auction was exceptional for its completeness, for its being the entire contents of a moving van. In her last years, after the Miller marriage ended, she had bought herself a small house in Los Angeles and was living on her own. These were the furnishings of a diminished life, many of the items no better than you would find at a yard sale anywhere in America. She had bought herself a few expensive dresses, confirming her true size, 35–22–35. There were bustiers, and some lingerie, but not much underwear. 'She loathed wearing panties,' one of her biographers wrote. She had kept the wedding ring Joe DiMaggio had given her, which she had worn for the nine months of that marriage; she had a signed baseball. She was a magpie in her saving – the shoes she wore to entertain the troops in Korea in 1954, the harem costume she wore for a 1958 *Life* magazine shoot, even a detailed diet folded into a cookbook.

Marilyn's library, containing many cookbooks, was that of a well-intentioned self-improver, most of the books in mint condition, obviously unread; others not only obviously read but also scribbled in. Some, such as volumes by John Huston and Clifford Odets, were inscribed. She had taken courses at UCLA when she was twenty-five to try to educate herself. It is hard to imagine what acquaintance Marilyn might have had with James Joyce's *Ulysses* or Marx's *Capital*, Tolstoy or Dostoevsky; but it is known that she was familiar with Khalil Gibran and *The Little Prince*, and in Lot 547 there was a copy of Harold Robbins's *The Carpetbaggers*. Her last secretary is on the record as saying, 'I never saw her read anything, except once, Harold Robbins.'

The books – titles, jackets, date of publication – were of a period, and the rest of the assortment of the same period; the whole of it like the contents of a time capsule of the 1950s: a Magnavox fifteen-inch black-and-white TV, Capri pants, baby-doll nightdresses, *The Joy of Cooking*, generic rather than designer blue jeans, cat-eye-style horn-rimmed glasses, mirrored bedside tables, a satin headboard, an armchair in black leatherette – 'leatherette' alone is a time-warp word. The mirrored side tables were smashed. The satin-covered headboard for her double bed was dusty and faded; the leatherette was torn. A clunky slide projector, enamelled cookware and copper kitchen utensils – including a potato masher and flour sifter – and much more all had the marks of use on them. A waste-paper basket, candlesticks, cheap Mexican pottery, two flip-top thumb-operated cigarette lighters.

In the event, each of these items went for thousands, and *The Joy of Cooking* (food stains and all) for $29,900.

But consider those cigarette lighters. They were gilt-metal, gift-boxed and had raised lettering: 'FRANK SINATRA'S CAL-NEVA LODGE'. Such a lot has a certain value for its associations, but in terms of Marilyn's life the associations are full of significance. Sinatra was one of Marilyn's lovers; the lodge had been bankrolled by the mobster Sam Giancana, one of whose mistresses, Judith Campbell, like Marilyn, had been the lover of President Kennedy. Old Joe Kennedy used to visit Cal-Neva. The gangster Skinny D'Amato, also the manager of Cal-Neva, was a boon companion of Joe DiMaggio, who also spent time gambling there. Marilyn, desperately bingeing, was often accompanied to the lodge by Peter Lawford, the Kennedys' facilitator, not to say pimp. Marilyn spent the last weekend of her life at Cal-Neva. Given all this, Lot 47, the Cal-Neva lighters, seem a repellent memento, representing the dark side of Marilyn's existence. The lighters sold for $48,300.

Studying these seemingly trivial objects, I felt I had been given a serious glimpse of Hollywood stardom; of the world of a lost soul. I grew up in the 1950s, and so it was also the world of my impressionable teens, when just a glimpse of Marilyn's bosom in a skimpy dress made me asthmatic with lust. The very ordinariness of the things said a great deal about Marilyn's life. It is one thing to read that Marilyn left school at fifteen, and, as an aspiring actress (one of the earliest fitness enthusiasts), exercised with weights, and was unhappily married to Arthur Miller. To see her childish misspelled handwriting, and the old-fashioned hand weights, and the 'Certificate of Conversion' to the Jewish faith and the sheet of paper mono-grammed MMM, blank except for the words in her writing pencilled on one line 'He does not love me', is quite another.

Now this coherent collection is entirely dispersed. Because it has been broken up, each separate part of it has become a fetish object, open to interpretation, part of a new mythology.

POCKET PENGUINS

1. Lady Chatterley's Trial
2. **Eric Schlosser** Cogs in the Great Machine
3. **Nick Hornby** Otherwise Pandemonium
4. **Albert Camus** Summer in Algiers
5. **P. D. James** Innocent House
6. **Richard Dawkins** The View from Mount Improbable
7. **India Knight** On Shopping
8. **Marian Keyes** Nothing Bad Ever Happens in Tiffany's
9. **Jorge Luis Borges** The Mirror of Ink
10. **Roald Dahl** A Taste of the Unexpected
11. **Jonathan Safran Foer** The Unabridged Pocketbook of Lightning
12. **Homer** The Cave of the Cyclops
13. **Paul Theroux** Two Stars
14. **Elizabeth David** Of Pageants and Picnics
15. **Anaïs Nin** Artists and Models
16. **Antony Beevor** Christmas at Stalingrad
17. **Gustave Flaubert** The Desert and the Dancing Girls
18. **Anne Frank** The Secret Annexe
19. **James Kelman** Where I Was
20. **Hari Kunzru** Noise
21. **Simon Schama** The Bastille Falls
22. **William Trevor** The Dressmaker's Child
23. **George Orwell** In Defence of English Cooking
24. **Michael Moore** Idiot Nation
25. **Helen Dunmore** Rose, 1944
26. **J. K. Galbraith** The Economics of Innocent Fraud
27. **Gervase Phinn** The School Inspector Calls
28. **W. G. Sebald** Young Austerlitz
29. **Redmond O'Hanlon** Borneo and the Poet
30. **Ali Smith** Ali Smith's Supersonic 70s
31. **Sigmund Freud** Forgetting Things
32. **Simon Armitage** King Arthur in the East Riding
33. **Hunter S. Thompson** Happy Birthday, Jack Nicholson
34. **Vladimir Nabokov** Cloud, Castle, Lake
35. **Niall Ferguson** 1914: Why the World Went to War

36. **Muriel Spark** The Snobs
37. **Steven Pinker** Hotheads
38. **Tony Harrison** Under the Clock
39. **John Updike** Three Trips
40. **Will Self** Design Faults in the Volvo 760 Turbo
41. **H. G. Wells** The Country of the Blind
42. **Noam Chomsky** Doctrines and Visions
43. **Jamie Oliver** Something for the Weekend
44. **Virginia Woolf** Street Haunting
45. **Zadie Smith** Martha and Hanwell
46. **John Mortimer** The Scales of Justice
47. **F. Scott Fitzgerald** The Diamond as Big as the Ritz
48. **Roger McGough** The State of Poetry
49. **Ian Kershaw** Death in the Bunker
50. **Gabriel García Márquez** Seventeen Poisoned Englishmen
51. **Steven Runciman** The Assault on Jerusalem
52. **Sue Townsend** The Queen in Hell Close
53. **Primo Levi** Iron Potassium Nickel
54. **Alistair Cooke** Letters from Four Seasons
55. **William Boyd** Protobiography
56. **Robert Graves** Caligula
57. **Melissa Bank** The Worst Thing a Suburban Girl Could Imagine
58. **Truman Capote** My Side of the Matter
59. **David Lodge** Scenes of Academic Life
60. **Anton Chekhov** The Kiss
61. **Claire Tomalin** Young Bysshe
62. **David Cannadine** The Aristocratic Adventurer
63. **P. G. Wodehouse** Jeeves and the Impending Doom
64. **Franz Kafka** The Great Wall of China
65. **Dave Eggers** Short Short Stories
66. **Evelyn Waugh** The Coronation of Haile Selassie
67. **Pat Barker** War Talk
68. **Jonathan Coe** 9th & 13th
69. **John Steinbeck** Murder
70. **Alain de Botton** On Seeing and Noticing